ZAPATO POWER
FREDDIE RAMOS
GETS A SIDEKICK

JACQUELINE JULES   art by KEIRON WARD

Albert Whitman & Company
Chicago, Illinois

Don't miss the first nine **Zapato Power** books!

Freddie Ramos Takes Off
Freddie Ramos Springs into Action
Freddie Ramos Zooms to the Rescue
Freddie Ramos Makes a Splash
Freddie Ramos Stomps the Snow
Freddie Ramos Rules New York
Freddie Ramos Hears It All
Freddie Ramos Adds It All Up
Freddie Ramos Tracks Down a Drone

Library of Congress Cataloging-in-Publication
data is on file with the publisher.
Text copyright © 2020 by Jacqueline Jules
Illustrations copyright © 2020 by Albert Whitman & Company
Illustrations by Keiron Ward
Hardcover edition first published in the United States of America
in 2020 by Albert Whitman & Company
Paperback edition first published in the United States of America
in 2021 by Albert Whitman & Company
ISBN 978-0-8075-9567-1 (paperback)
ISBN 978-0-8075-9566-4 (ebook)

Printed in the United States of America

10 9 8 7 6 5 4 3 2 1 LB 24 23 22 21 20

Design by Valerie Hernández

For more information about Albert Whitman & Company,
visit our website at www.albertwhitman.com.

To teachers and librarians. Thank you for the hard work you do on behalf of children everywhere.
—JJ

Contents

1. My Goggles Are Missing

The sky was blue. The grass was green. The air was in-between. Not too hot and not too cold. It was a perfect day for running fast! *¡Muy rápido!* I stood by the overhead train track behind my home, Starwood Park Apartments, feeling a smile on my face. My favorite thing to do after a long day at school was to race the train in my super-powered purple sneakers.

I reached into my pocket for my silver goggles. My smile disappeared. Where were my goggles? They weren't in my jeans, and I needed them to protect my eyes when I zoomed ninety miles an hour. Did they fall out again? This was the second time in two days!

I touched my purple wristband to turn on my super speed. If I retraced my steps, maybe I could find them.

ZOOM! ZOOM! ZAPATO!

My silver goggles were not on
the sidewalk. Were they on the
stairs going down to Starwood
Elementary? I was just about to
search when I heard a voice.

"Freddie!"

Gio, my first-grade neighbor, was calling me. This was not a good time. I wanted to find my goggles so I could have fun racing the train.

"FREDDIE!" Gio called again.

A superhero should always help others first. I hurried back to Building G, where Gio was waving his arms.

"Puppy is missing!" Gio said.

"¿Otra vez?" I asked.

Puppy was lost yesterday too.

"You should use a leash," I told him.

"I do!" Gio said. "Puppy pulled it out of my hands when I stopped to tie my shoe."

Gio's dog liked to chase squirrels. You needed super speed to keep up with a dog who kept running off.

ZOOM! ZOOM! ZAPATO!

I took off in a cloud of invisible smoke.

Luckily, Puppy hadn't run too far away. But I found the other thing I was looking for in Puppy's mouth. My silver goggles! Ugh!

"Give those back!" I told Puppy.

Puppy was not a good listener. He wouldn't drop my goggles until Gio came over with a doggy treat. By then, they were too slobbery to put on my face. Yuck!

"*Lo siento*," Gio said. "Puppy likes to chew things."

"And run off," I added.

"He's not as fast you." Gio sighed. "I wish I was."

Gio was always saying that. He wanted to vanish in a puff of smoke the way I did.

"Do you think I'll get faster when I'm bigger?" Gio asked.

"Sure," I said. "Eat vegetables. My mom says they make you grow."

"Thanks, Freddie!"

Gio left with Puppy, and I headed over to see my friend, Mr. Vaslov, with my drippy goggles. I held them by the strap so I didn't have to touch dog slobber.

Mr. Vaslov opened his toolshed

door. "What happened, Freddie?"

I told him how Puppy had found my goggles before I could.

He handed me a towel to wipe them off.

"It sounds like you need a tracker for those goggles."

"Can you make one?" I asked.

Mr. Vaslov invented my super-powered purple sneakers and the wristband that controls my super speed, super bounce, and super hearing. Compared to that, a tracker sounded easy.

"I could." Mr. Vaslov blinked behind his wire glasses. "And so could you, Freddie."

Me? Could I be an inventor too? *¡Qué buena idea!*

"Let's get started!"

"Tomorrow," Mr. Vaslov said. "Today, I'm finishing another project."

"What?" I looked at Mr. Vaslov's

worktable and saw my first pair
of purple shoes with silver wings
on the side. They were too small
for my feet now. Was Mr. Vaslov
fixing them to give super speed to
someone else?

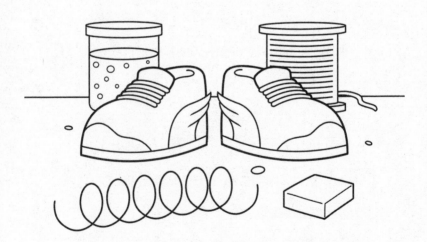

2. The Smaller Shoes

Mr. Vaslov pointed at the small sneakers. "They're almost ready for a new owner."

When Mr. Vaslov made bigger shoes for me, he put the smaller ones on a shelf in his toolshed. Why couldn't they stay there? Starwood Park didn't need two superheroes.

"Zapato Power is a big responsibility," I said. "Are you sure you want to give special shoes to someone else?"

Mr. Vaslov smiled. "I took a chance when I picked you, and it turned out all right."

"Why did you pick me?" I asked.

He counted on his fingers. "First, I saw how much you liked running."

I grinned. Even before I had Zapato Power, I used to race the train, just for fun.

"Second," Mr. Vaslov said, "I thought you were someone I could

12

trust, not someone who would brag about having superpowers or use them to hurt, rather than help, people."

Mr. Vaslov was right about me. But was there really another kid at Starwood Park he could trust?

"Third—" He lifted a purple shoe from the worktable. It looked small compared to mine now. "Back then, your feet were just the right size for these!"

"So you're looking

for someone who is responsible and has small feet," I said.

"Yes!" Mr. Vaslov laughed. "Do you have any suggestions?"

Hmmm. Some superheroes had partners. Batman had Robin. If I chose the person who got the smaller shoes, then maybe it wouldn't be so bad.

"Can I think about it?" I asked Mr. Vaslov. "I don't want to pick the wrong person."

"Hold on, Freddie." Mr. Vaslov held up his hand. "You won't be making the final choice. You'll just be helping."

There were lots of kids at Starwood Park with small feet. Deciding wouldn't be easy. Maybe Mr. Vaslov would give up and put the shoes back on the shelf.

"Come over tomorrow, Freddie." Mr. Vaslov walked me to the door. "We'll discuss making a tracker that works with your wristband."

I waved goodbye and went home to 29G.

WHEET! WHEET!

My guinea pig, Claude the Second, stood up in his cage to greet me. He was hungry.

WHEET! WHEET!

I opened the refrigerator to take out a bag of baby carrots. Claude the Second ate two and so did I.

When Mom came home from work with her boyfriend, David, she saw me and my guinea pig chomping away.

"¡*Cómo me encanta!*" Mom

kissed my cheek. "My son eating vegetables! This is what I like to see."

My mom also

likes seeing me eat lasagna and being nice to David. Before Mom started dating David, we never ate lasagna. Since he started coming for dinner, we'd eaten it a lot.

"How was school, Freddie?" David asked as we sat down.

Why did grown-ups always ask kids about their day? I could never remember the boring parts, and the exciting parts weren't easy to explain.

Mom had said I should look at David's face and do the best I could.

"My day was fine," I said. "We learned cartwheels in gym."

David smiled, showing all his teeth. He seemed happy that I talked to him. Mom looked happy too. It was weird how grown-ups liked to know what kids did in school. It was also weird how

I was getting used to eating lasagna
and having David over for dinner
every night.

The next morning, I zipped my
goggles into my backpack before
I left for Starwood Elementary. I
didn't want to take any chances
with my pockets before I had a
tracker. On the way, I stopped by
Mr. Vaslov's toolshed to say hello.
He wasn't alone.

Gio was inside talking to him.

"Purple shoes with wings on the

side!" Gio pointed at Mr. Vaslov's worktable. "They look just like Freddie's!"

Mr. Vaslov winked at me. What did that mean? Did Mr. Vaslov think Gio should have super speed?

3. Another First Grader

I had to get Gio out of there before
Mr. Vaslov made a huge mistake.
Gio wasn't responsible. He couldn't
take care of Zapato Power shoes!
He couldn't even take care of his
dog!

And Gio was a big talker. He
thought it was his job to tell
everybody everything he knew.

The whole neighborhood had heard about my mom's boyfriend from Gio. Mr. Vaslov couldn't trust Gio to be quiet about super shoes with super speed.

"Let's go to school!" I grabbed Gio's hand and pulled him out of the toolshed.

"What's the hurry, Freddie?" Gio asked.

We went down the steps to the school and through the playground. It was so early, there was only one other student there. A girl in Gio's class named Amy Escobar. She was walking slowly

with her eyes down, like she was searching for something.

"Did you see my sunglasses?" Amy asked.

"The pink ones?" Gio answered.

Outside of school, we always saw Amy in sunglasses. She liked to wear them even more than I liked to wear goggles.

"Yes!" she said. "You found them?"

"No," Gio said, "but I know what they look like."

"Oh." Amy's face fell.

"Ask Freddie to look," Gio said. "He found my dog yesterday."

"Will you?" Amy asked. "They're somewhere outside. Maybe up at Starwood Park."

Did I have enough time before the bell? With my super shoes, I could be back in two blinks.

ZOOM! ZOOM! ZAPATO!

A pair of pink sunglasses were on the ground by Building C, where Amy lived.

ZOOM! ZOOM! ZAPATO!

"Thanks, Freddie!" Amy's face

lit up when I came back.

Real superhero jobs didn't happen too often at elementary school. Most of the time I used my super speed for bringing back lost stuff. That was okay. I liked seeing people smile.

The rest of the day was nice. We didn't have any tests, lunch was beef tacos, and in gym, Mr. Gooley let us do cartwheels and handstands.

"Look at me!" Maria said. "I did two in a row!"

Maria was my partner for gymnastics. She was also Gio's

older sister and my next door
neighbor. We did a lot of things
together. I thought about telling
Mr. Vaslov that IF he had to give
the small Zapato Power shoes to
someone, Maria would be better
than Gio. Then I remembered
Maria's feet were too big, like mine.

"How many cartwheels can you do, Freddie?" she asked.

Maria challenged me until Mr. Gooley blew the whistle.

"Practice on your own," Mr. Gooley said as we left class.

"We will," Maria promised.

After school, I went to the overhead track behind Starwood Park. I wanted to race the train and make up for yesterday, when all my running had been about a lost dog and lost goggles.

I stopped short.

Somebody had beat me there. Amy was waiting on the grass,

wearing her pink sunglasses, with
her arms out like the wings of
an airplane. As soon as the train
rumbled by, she started running.

"Does that look familiar?" a deep
voice asked.

Mr. Vaslov was behind me.

He was sitting on his red electric scooter—the one he used to get around Starwood Park when his bad knee was bothering him. We watched Amy together.

"She likes to run, just like you do," Mr. Vaslov said.

Was Mr. Vaslov thinking of another first grader for the small Zapato Power shoes? A girl who wore pink sunglasses? Not Gio?

I didn't want to ask. If I asked, it might help Mr. Vaslov decide. And I didn't want him to make up his mind yet.

Right now, I was the only one

who helped Mr. Vaslov do his job of taking care of Starwood Park. If someone else had super-powered shoes, Mr. Vaslov wouldn't need me. I wouldn't be special anymore.

4. What Happened to the Fence?

Mr. Vaslov and I went back to his toolshed to start work on my goggle tracker.

"Okay, Freddie," Mr. Vaslov said. "Let's identify the problem."

That was easy. My goggles kept falling out of my pocket and getting lost.

"What is the solution?"

"We make a tracker so I can find them," I said.

"And how do you want it to work?"

I scratched my head. "Could it make a noise, so I'd know where my goggles are?"

"Do you want a loud sound or a soft sound?"

Why did I have to answer so many questions before I got started?

"An invention needs a plan," Mr. Vaslov explained.

"It's part of the process."

Scientists like to be organized and do things step by step. If I wanted to be scientific, I had to use some brain power.

"Let's look at your wristband, Freddie."

We examined the buttons. There was one for super speed and one for super bounce. To get super hearing, I rubbed both of them until they got warm.

"Could we add a button?" I asked.

"A big one or a little one?" Mr. Vaslov asked.

Making decisions was hard work. By the time I left the toolshed, I needed a run to clear my mind.

ZOOM! ZOOM! ZAPATO!

Finally, the space by the overhead track was free. No Amy. No Gio. No lost Puppy. Only me, the grass, and the train rumbling by.

ZOOM! ZOOM! ZaPaTO!

I spread out my arms, pretending to be an airplane.

ZOOM! ZOOM! ZaPaTO!

I raced to the station and back.

It would have been great if I'd been as alone as I thought.

"Freddie?" Amy asked. "Is that you?"

She was standing right there, when I stepped out of a puff of smoke.

"Have you seen my sunglasses?"

Again? Amy's sunglasses were like Gio's dog—always missing. Mr. Vaslov shouldn't give Amy super speed, either. The smaller shoes should stay on a shelf forever.

"Could you help me look?" Amy asked.

Amy went in one direction, and I went in the other.

ZOOM! ZOOM! ZAPATO!

Her sunglasses were not on the sidewalk or the stairs. I tried the grass near Building F. Lots of kids

played there because a wooden
fence protected that side of
Starwood Park from a busy street.

ZOOM!ZOOM!ZAPATO!

I searched for something pink
sticking out of the grass. No luck.

Then I looked
closer to the
fence. Instead of
sunglasses, I found
something strange.
Holes in the fence.
Mr. Vaslov liked
everything at

Starwood Park to look nice. He would want me to investigate this.

I counted. There were four holes, as round as nickels and deep. Why would someone put holes in the fence?

And where were Amy's sunglasses?

"Freddie!" Amy waved from the sidewalk. "I found them."

Amy was happy. But I was still puzzled about the fence. Should I talk to Mr. Vaslov?

My stomach was growling. I decided to go home for dinner first.

"*Lávate las manos*," Mom said. "We're eating soon."

"Where's David?" I asked as soon as my hands were clean.

"It's Thursday night," Mom said.

Last week, David told us he would be busy on Thursday nights for a while. He said it was a surprise.

The table felt empty with only two people. I could hear the clock ticking on the wall. Mom was lost in her thoughts, and so was I.

Who put the holes in the fence by Building F? Could I wait to tell Mr. Vaslov? If I fixed things myself, Mr. Vaslov would see I was the only hero Starwood Park needed. Maybe he would change his mind about giving someone else Zapato Power shoes.

After all, wasn't it better for only one kid to have super speed? Me.

5. The Hole in My Door

Friday morning, the doorbell rang as I was finishing breakfast. Mom ran to answer it.

"David!" Her voice sounded like she was singing, the way it always did around him.

His voice sounded worried. "Rosa, come outside. You need to

see something."

"*¿Qué?*" I heard Mom's voice through the open door. "*¿Qué pasó aquí?*"

Mom only spoke Spanish to David when she was excited. I left my cereal to see what was going on.

There was a perfectly shaped hole, the size of a nickel, on the door beside the knob. It looked like the holes in the fence by Building F.

"Who would drill a hole in your door?" David asked.

"A robber?" Mom said.

David looked more closely at
the hole. "It's deep, but it doesn't
go all the way through."

"Is that important?" I asked.

"I'm not sure," David said, "at least no one can look through this hole into your house."

So the hole wasn't for spying or breaking in. What else could it be for? Was this hole connected to the ones in the fence?

Mom picked up her purse. "David is driving me to work, and we don't want to be late. Can you tell Mr. Vaslov about this hole, Freddie?"

I nodded because I planned to tell Mr. Vaslov the second I figured it all out.

When David's blue car drove off,

I touched my purple wristband.

ZOOM! ZOOM! Zapato!

The first thing I did was check
the fence. The four holes were still
there, plus three more.

Starwood Park must have
someone with a drill. I'd seen Mr.
Vaslov use one. His drill made
a buzzing sound and left bits of
sawdust behind, just like I was
seeing now. Who was the driller?
Were there other holes around
Starwood Park?

ZOOM! ZOOM! ZAPATO!

I raced around the buildings.
My Zapato Power smoke gave me
sharp vision, like someone looking
through binoculars. I spotted two
more doors in Building G with
holes in them. Building H had
window frames with holes. The
driller had been very busy!

Who was it? A person with a
tool? Or something else? Once
I saw a scary movie with a giant
flying robot that drilled holes
everywhere. Remembering that

movie made me want to be sure I could get out of the way quick. I pressed my wristband to test my super bounce.

BOING! BOING! BOING!

My super shoes let me jump
high enough to see the roof of any
building at Starwood Park. I was
ready for a scary robot. Except I
didn't have time. School was about
to start. Superheroes need to know
things so they can make good
decisions. And I couldn't be smart
if I didn't go to class.

I reached my seat in Mrs.
Blaine's classroom a second before
the tardy bell rang. I was tired. It
had already been a busy morning.

After lunch, we went to the playground. Maria wanted to practice cartwheels.

"Let's have a race!"

I liked flipping upside down and whirling like a wheel across the grass. In gym, Mr. Gooley made us stay on the mats, and he made us stop if we got too wild. On the playground, Maria and I could be as wild as we wanted.

Jasmin was watching from a bench nearby. Maria asked her to join us. Soon, there were three sets of legs flying in the air close together, near the bench.

"Watch out!" Maria shouted.

I swerved so my foot wouldn't hit Jasmin's head. BOOM! My foot hit the bench instead.

"OW!" I screamed.

Maria plopped down beside me. "Are you hurt?"

"YES!" I grabbed my foot and moaned.

"We'll take you to the nurse!" Jasmin said.

Maria and Jasmin let me lean on them while I hopped slowly to Mrs. Cole's office. They didn't complain about how many times I said "OUCH!"

Mrs. Cole was nice too. She took off my sneaker very gently so she could look at my foot. I looked too, and I didn't like what I saw.

My ankle was as purple as my shoe!

6. Big Blue Boot

Mom came to my school with David.

"*Mi hijito.*" Mom stroked my cheek. "Don't worry. We're here."

David carried me so I didn't have to hop with a hurt ankle. He drove us to the hospital in his blue car. It was different having two grown-ups with me. My dad was a soldier who died a long time ago. I'd never had anybody but my mom to take care of me before.

"Hang in there, Freddie," David said. "It should only be a little while longer."

Hospitals are not places where things happen fast. We waited to see a doctor. We waited for an X-ray. We waited for results.

"Would you like a peppermint?" David asked.

"How about some water?" Mom asked.

Mom and David did their best to keep me busy. It sort of worked. I only thought about my Zapato Power some of the time, not all of it. Mom had put my left sneaker in her giant handbag, so I knew it was safe. What I didn't know was how soon I'd be able to run again.

"Six to eight weeks," the doctor said as she fitted a big blue boot on my foot. "Your ankle is broken and needs time to heal."

The thought of not running for so many weeks felt terrible. A few tears leaked from my eyes.

Mom hugged me. David touched my back.

"*Lo siento*," he said.

What? David told me he was sorry in Spanish. I thought he didn't speak Spanish like Mom and I did. Were there things about David I didn't know?

By the time we got home, we were all hungry. Mom ordered pizza, and David helped me get comfortable with some pillows on the couch. He also gave my guinea pig, Claude the Second, a carrot.

Then Mr. Vaslov called.

"Gio told me about the cartwheel accident," he said. "Are you okay?"

"I have to wear a big blue boot," I told Mr. Vaslov, "and use crutches."

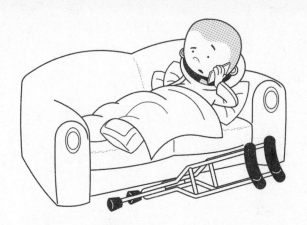

"It won't be forever," he said.

"It will feel like forever," I answered.

"We'll work on your goggle tracker," Mr. Vaslov said. "You don't need to run fast to be an inventor."

But I did need Zapato Power to be a hero. Who would find Gio's dog? Or Amy's sunglasses?

And how could I find out who was drilling holes at Starwood Park? I still wanted to solve that mystery myself and show Mr. Vaslov he only needed one kid with super-powered shoes.

On Saturday, Mr. Vaslov and I worked in his toolshed. We put a new button on my wristband and an electronic chip in my goggles.

"Now they can communicate with each other," Mr. Vaslov said.

"Should we test it?" I asked.

Mr. Vaslov nodded. "Let's go outside."

I put my goggles on the grass and walked away on crutches. I could move, just not very fast.

"Press the new button on your wristband," Mr. Vaslov said.

RUFF! RUFF! RUFF!

What was that? Was Puppy loose again? No! My goggles were making that sound. They were barking like a dog. And Mrs. Flores was passing by on the sidewalk with her beagle. He started barking too.

"This is too much noise," I told Mr. Vaslov.

"You're right," he agreed. "We need to program the electronic chip to make a different sound."

Mr. Vaslov explained trial and error. It meant that the first time inventors tried something, it didn't always work the way they expected.

"Inventors don't give up," Mr. Vaslov said. "They keep trying until they get it right."

We went back inside the

toolshed. Mr. Vaslov asked me to sit down on one of his stools. He sat down too.

"Let's talk about the small Zapato Power shoes," he said. "I think Amy should get them."

7. Amy Is Brave

I shook my head. "Amy loses
stuff. She's not responsible."

"You lose your goggles," Mr.
Vaslov reminded me.

Oops! That's why we were
making a tracker.

"Are you sure you need two
kids with super speed?" I asked.

Mr. Vaslov rubbed his bad knee, the one that made it hard for him to walk across Starwood Park. With my foot in a boot, he would only have his electric scooter for help.

"Is it because I broke my ankle?" I asked.

"No," Mr. Vaslov said. "Amy is a brave girl. She will put the small shoes to good use."

Bullies bothered Amy when she first came to Starwood Park. She learned to stand up for herself and make friends.

"Amy would help others, like

you do," Mr. Vaslov said.

Mr. Vaslov was usually right about people. I wished I felt so sure.

"Can I call her?" Mr. Vaslov picked up his phone.

I didn't want to say yes, but I didn't have a good reason to say no.

When Amy arrived, we showed her the small Zapato Power shoes and told her what they could do.

She jumped up and down. "Can I try them?"

Mr. Vaslov looked at me. "Amy needs a teacher."

For the second time that day, I didn't have a good reason to say no.

I took Amy to the place beside
the overhead track to practice.
She zipped back and forth at least
twenty times.

"I feel like a rocket!" She laughed.

ZIP! ZIP! ZAPATO

Amy's shoes didn't work exactly

like mine. Mr. Vaslov had made a
silver wristband with one button
to control hers. She didn't have
super hearing or super bounce,
only super speed.

ZIP! ZIP! ZaPaTO!

Amy zoomed past me in a cloud
of Zapato Power smoke. She was
as fast as a flash of light. Was that
what I looked like when I ran?
Cool!

When she stopped to rest, I
explained a few more things.

"The smoke comes out of your

heels," I said, "and it makes you invisible."

"Does it help me see better too?" Amy asked. "I feel like I'm wearing binoculars."

"Yes." I nodded. "I call that Zapato Power eyes."

"Awesome!" Amy smiled. "So tell me what I can do. I want a superhero job."

Amy wasn't the only one who wanted to do superhero stuff. But she was the only one right now who could run around and find out who was drilling holes at Starwood Park.

ZIP! ZIP! Zapato!

She took off the second I asked. Now I knew what it was like to be a teacher who told kids what to do.

ZIP! ZIP! Zapato!

Amy came back a few minutes later with a report.

"There are ten holes in the fence now, and two in your front door."

"Two in my door?" I repeated.

We went back to 29G and examined the holes together.

"Who would do this?" Amy wondered.

"Could it be a giant flying robot?" I asked.

"I hope not." Amy put her eye near one of the holes.

"Something's moving in there!" She stepped back.

BUZZ! BUZZ! BUZZ!

"A bee!" Amy shouted.

She could have run away and left me stuck on crutches with my big blue boot. Instead, she stood right beside me as the bee flew over our heads and around the building.

"What's a bee doing in your door?" she asked.

We needed a grown-up to understand this. It was time to go inside and call Mr. Vaslov. He came over a few minutes later on his red electric scooter.

"It's a carpenter bee," Mr. Vaslov said. "They spread pollen and help plants the way other bees do."

"Other bees live in hives," Amy

said. "And make honey."

"Not these," Mr. Vaslov said. "They make nests in wood, and sometimes they damage houses."

"Does that mean we have to stop them?" I asked.

Mr. Vaslov sighed. "We have to protect the buildings."

"We can't kill bees!" Amy cried. "They help flowers grow!"

Amy was right. I learned about that in school. Bees needed to be protected too. How could we save the bees and Starwood Park?

8. A Good Team

It was Saturday night, not
Thursday, so David was having
dinner with Mom and me. He
wanted to know how my first day
in the blue walking boot was.

"Busy!" I said. "I solved a
mystery!"

Mom wasn't exactly glad to hear

there were bees living in our front door.

"Do they sting?" Mom asked.

"Mr. Vaslov said most of them don't. Carpenter bees are not the same as bumblebees."

"Do they look alike?" David asked.

"I'm not sure," I said.

"We should learn more," David said after dinner. "Let's look them up."

He turned on Mom's laptop, and we did a search on the internet until we found some pictures.

"Carpenter bees aren't fuzzy like

bumblebees," David said. "Their
bodies are black and shiny."

Knowing the difference between
carpenter bees and other bees was
important. Except it didn't solve
the problem at Starwood Park.

"How do we make them

want to live somewhere else?" I asked David.

David started typing. "Let's find out!"

The first website we found said we should use poison.

"That's not safe for the bees or us," I told David.

"*Tienes razón,*" David said.

I was glad to hear David agreeing with me. I just didn't expect him to say it in Spanish.

"*¿Hablas español?*" I asked.

"I'm taking a class," David explained, "to surprise your mom."

So that's where he went on

Thursday nights. If David was learning Spanish for my mom, he must really like her. Did that mean I might be getting a new dad one day?

"Mom thinks it's good to know more than one language," I said.

"*Sí,*" David said. "She's right!"

We smiled at each other before going back to our internet search.

"Look!" I said. "There's a safer way to make carpenter bees go away."

I couldn't wait to tell Mr. Vaslov and Amy.

In the morning, I went to the toolshed with a spray bottle that smelled like lemons. I explained how it worked.

"This isn't poison. It won't hurt the bees. They just don't like the smell of citrus fruit."

"Brilliant!" Mr. Vaslov said. "They will leave on their own before I fill the holes and paint."

I felt full of brain power. I'd figured out how to save the bees and Starwood Park. So I was only a little sad when Mr. Vaslov called Amy for a job that needed super speed.

"Can you run around the buildings and spray every hole you see?"

"Absolutely!" Amy said.

ZIP! ZIP! ZaPaTO!

While Amy was gone, Mr. Vaslov and I worked on my goggle tracker. We talked about the new sound I wanted in place of the barking dog.

"Is that all you want to change?" Mr. Vaslov asked.

I decided it would also be good for the button to have a flashing arrow that pointed in the direction of my goggles.

"This way, I can know which way to go," I told Mr. Vaslov.

"Inventive thinking!" Mr. Vaslov approved. "And we have the equipment and the software to program this change."

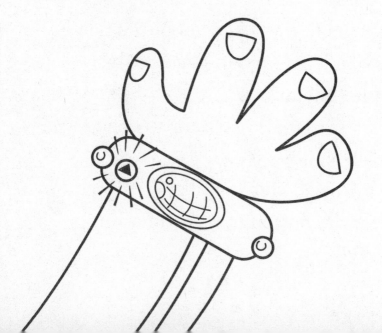

Amy came back to the toolshed just as we were going outside for a test. She wanted to help.

"Can you drop my goggles behind one of the buildings?" I asked.

"Sure!"

ZIP! ZIP! ZAPATO!

Now we were ready. I pressed the new button on my wristband. We followed the arrow down the sidewalk and behind Building C, until we heard my goggles.

BUZZ! BUZZ! BUZZ!

Mr. Vaslov winked at me. "A bee sound is much better than a bark."

Amy was waiting for us, standing beside my goggles. My invention worked perfectly.

"Wow!" Amy said. "Can you make a tracker for me? My sunglasses are lost. They fell off while I was running."

Mr. Vaslov patted my back. "What do you think, Freddie?"

I was glad I had invented something both Amy and I needed. We were going to make a good team.

Don't Miss Freddie's Other Adventures!

One day Freddie Ramos comes home from school and finds a strange box just for him. What's inside?

HC 978-0-8075-9480-3
PB 978-0-8075-9479-7

In this sequel, Freddie has shoes that give him super speed. It's hard to be a superhero and a regular kid at the same time, especially when your shoes give you even more power!

PB 978-0-8075-9483-4

Freddie's super-speedy adventures continue—now he has superhero duties at school!

PB 978-0-8075-9484-1

When Freddie's zapatos go missing, how can he use his Zapato Power?

HC 978-0-8075-9485-8
PB 978-0-8075-9486-5

There's a blizzard in Starwood Park—but the weather can't stop a thief! It's up to Freddie and his Zapato Power to save the day!

HC 978-0-8075-9487-2
PB 978-0-8075-9496-4

What happens when Freddie outgrows his zapatos?

HC 978-0-8075-9497-1
PB 978-0-8075-9499-5

How will Freddie learn to use his new super hearing without becoming a super snoop?

HC 978-0-8075-9500-8
PB 978-0-8075-9542-8

Freddie's failing math and trying to protect a new girl at school—but his Zapato Power is no help! What will Freddie do?

HC 978-0-8075-9539-8
PB 978-0-8075-9559-6

Mr. Vaslov is building a drone to help him take care of Starwood Park—but that's Freddie's job! And when Freddie finds out his mom has a new boyfriend, he's worried about their relationship too. How can his Zapato Power help with all this change?

HC 978-0-8075-9544-2
PB 978-0-8075-9563-3

Jacqueline Jules is the author of more than forty books, including *Freddie Ramos Takes Off*, a Cybils Award winner. She lives in northern Virginia, just outside Washington, DC. Visit her at www.jacquelinejules.com.

Keiron Ward has always loved drawing his favorite heroes and villains. He lives in Wales.